Jenny Valentine

Iggy & Me

and the

HAPPY BIRTHDAY

Also by Jenny Valentine

Iggy and Me

# Jenny Valentine

# Iggy & Me

## and the

# HAPPY BIRTHDAY

## Illustrated by Joe Berger

HarperCollins *Children's Books*

First published in Great Britain by HarperCollins
*Children's Books* in 2010
HarperCollins *Children's Books* is a division of
HarperCollins *Publishers* Ltd
77-85 Fulham Palace Road, Hammersmith, London W6 8JB

www.harpercollins.co.uk

1

ISBN: 978-0-00-728363 7

Printed and bound in England by
Clays Ltd, St Ives plc

# Contents

# Iggy the fish

My name is Flo and I have a little sister called
Iggy.

Iggy was learning to swim. Dad said she was
taking her time about it. This was because Iggy
pretended to swim by walking about in the
shallow end and doing all the right things with
her arms.

"The top half has got it," said Dad, "but somebody forgot to tell the legs."

Iggy didn't think her legs needed to be told.

"Look," she said. "Swimming is *easy*." And she hopped from one foot to the other and flapped her arms about.

Dad said she looked like a duck coming in to land.

Mum said, "Iggy, that isn't swimming."

"Yes it is," Iggy said.

I was keeping out of it.

On the way home on the bus, Iggy was falling asleep. Dad said she was tired from all her underwater running.

"I'm not tired," Iggy said, opening one eye and then closing it again. "And I wasn't running."

"What are we going to do with you?" said Mum. "How are we going to teach you to swim?"

"I *can* swim," Iggy said.

"Half of you can," Dad said. Iggy folded her arms and turned away.

"How did I learn to swim?" I said.

"We dropped you in the water when you were a baby," Dad said.

Iggy sniggered and then pretended it was a snore.

"Dad!" I said. "That's not very nice!"

"We didn't *drop* you," Mum said, elbowing Dad. "We were in the pool with you and we let you go."

"Is that allowed?" I said.

Mum said, "We went to special classes. We didn't just throw you in."

Dad said that all babies knew how to swim if you just dunked them in and helped them to remember.

Mum said, "Babies are surrounded by water when they're in the womb."

I looked at Mum's tummy. Iggy opened her eyes again.

"Why didn't you do that to Iggy?" I said.

"We tried," said Mum. "But she didn't like it."

"*You* didn't like it," said Dad.

"She was crying," Mum said.

"*Screaming*," said Dad.

"Iggy didn't take to it like you, Flo," said Mum. "You were a little fish."

Iggy sat up straight on the bus seat. She said, "I don't *want* to be a fish. Who'd want to be a *fish?*"

"Exactly," said Dad. "Who wants to be a fish when they can be a piglet?" And he tickled her until she snorted.

Later that week, Iggy had her first swimming lesson. I went with Mum to watch while Dad was at work.

It was in a secret, special pool that was hidden from all the other pools. You wouldn't know it was there. It was small and there was no deep end – you could stand *anywhere* in it. And the water was warm, nearly hot, like a bath.

There were four other people in Iggy's class:

+ a boy with Spider-man goggles and Incredible Hulk trunks;

◆ a girl with orange hair and an orange bikini, who cried and wouldn't look at the water;

◆ a girl with a special float-suit on that meant she couldn't sink, and which was probably cheating;

◆ and a boy from school called James, who was wearing pink armbands and looked even crosser than Iggy.

"I want to go home," Iggy said. "I don't like swimming lessons."

"You've never had one before," Mum said. "You might like it."

Iggy frowned and put her towel over her head. "I don't want one," she said.

"Too late," said Mum. "I just paid for six."

It was really hot in there with all our clothes on, and a bit funny-smelling, of pool water and other things. I took my coat off. The floor was wet so I had to keep it on my knee which was just as hot as wearing it. Everyone's mums and dads and brothers and sisters were sitting on a bench at the side of the room. We were waiting for the teacher.

The orange haired girl still wasn't looking at the water. The boy in the goggles was fiddling with his trunks.

James's mum was blowing up his armbands till they were too tight for him to take off. Iggy was hiding under her towel.

When the teacher came in she looked a bit like a mermaid. She had long wavy hair like mermaids do. She was wearing flip-flops and a red T-shirt that said LITTLE SPLASHERS on it in yellow writing. She got in the water with her T-shirt on.

Iggy appeared from under her towel at the sound of flip-flops. "Is she allowed to do that?" she said.

"I suppose so,' said Mum.

The teacher's name was Sasha. She called the class over to sit on the edge of the pool. The orange girl's mum had to go with her. You could see she was worried about her clothes getting wet.

"Let's see what you can do," Sasha said.

The orange girl did crying on dry land.

The floating girl did floating.

The boy with the goggles did splashing his brother.

James did doggy paddle and swallowing too much water.

And Iggy did running on the spot and flapping her arms.

"Very good," said Sasha.

Iggy looked at us and pulled a face that said, "See? I told you I could swim."

Sasha said, "Who can put their head underwater?"

Iggy ducked under and came back up again. "I told you so," her face said.

"Who can open their eyes down there?"

"Easy peasy," Iggy's smile said.

"Who can make their bottom float up to the surface?"

Iggy's smile disappeared. She looked at the others. Floating girl could. James could. The Incredible Hulk could.

Iggy couldn't. She lifted one leg, and then the other. One half of her bottom floated at a time, but not the whole thing.

"Oh dear," Mum said. "It's the moment of realisation."

"What's that mean?" I said.

"Iggy just found out she can't swim," said Mum.

Iggy's was frowning. She was biting her lip. Her face didn't say, "See?" any more. It said, "Help!"

"Come on, Iggy!" we said. "You can do it!"

Iggy's face said, "No I can't."

"Right," Sasha said to Iggy. "Let's have a look at you."

Iggy did balancing on one leg at a time.

Sasha put her hand under Iggy's tummy. Both her feet left the floor and her whole bottom did floating. Iggy looked very surprised.

"That," Sasha said, "is what swimming feels like. Have a go."

Iggy flapped her arms and legs about like a wild thing, while her teacher held her up.

"Perfect," said Sasha.

"Perfect," said Iggy in the changing room.

"Perfect," she said on the bus.

"Perfect," she said when Dad asked her how the lesson went.

"What was the teacher like?" he said.

"Perfect," Iggy said.

I said, "She looked like a mermaid."

"No she didn't," Iggy said.

"I think she did."

Iggy looked at me like I was crazy. She said, "Flo, mermaids don't have any *legs*."

Mum and Dad laughed.

I said, "I meant her hair mainly."

"Oh," she said.

"What did you do?" said Dad.

"*Swimming*, silly," Iggy said.

"Oh," said Dad. "How do you do 'swimming, silly'? Do you hop up and down and splash your top half about?"

Iggy looked cross, Mum said, "Stop it," and Dad said, "OK."

I was keeping out of it again.

"We did floating bottoms," Iggy said. "If you must know."

"What's a floating bottom?" said Dad.

Iggy giggled.

"How do you float a bottom?" Dad said. "I have to know."

Iggy said, "It's easy. You let go with your feet."

"Maybe you could show me next time we go swimming," Dad said.

Iggy said, "Can we go now?"

"Not now, Iggy," said Mum. "It's almost bedtime."

"Can we go tomorrow?" Iggy said.

"Maybe," said Mum. "I think we probably could."

"Good," said Iggy. "Then I can show all of you."

Iggy went to all six of her swimming lessons. Then she went to six more.

One day we were all swimming. Mum and Dad, and Iggy and me. I was being a mermaid and going underwater to find treasure. Dad threw his goggles for me and I dived down for them. They were the treasure.

Iggy was swimming along behind. Her feet weren't touching the bottom. Her legs were kicking and her arms were flapping and she was doing everything right. She swam up to Dad and held on to him to get her breath back.

"I've got bad news for you, Iggy," he said.

"What?" Iggy said. Her hair was all wet and peaky, and drops of water kept dripping in her eyes. "What?" she said again.

"You've turned into a *fish*," Dad said.

Iggy smiled. "It's better than being a piglet," she said, and she swam off, with her whole bottom floating, to find Mum.

# Iggy's birthday list

A long time before Iggy's birthday, we were all in the garden. Mum was digging and Dad was reading the newspaper. Iggy and me were putting food out for the birds.

"Mum and Dad," she said. "You know my birthday? Can I have a pet?"

Dad rustled his paper and Mum stopped digging.

Dad said, "What birthday?"

Mum said, "It's ages away."

"Is it?" Iggy said.

"*Ages*," said Dad, looking out from behind his paper.

Iggy drooped a little bit, but she carried on anyway.

"Well, when it's not ages away any more, can I have a pet? For my birthday?"

Mum and Dad smiled at each other. Dad shook his head.

"What sort of pet?" I asked.

"Just a small one," Iggy said. "Like a puppy or a kitten."

"Puppies and kittens grow into dogs and cats," said Dad.

"I know that, silly," she said.

"Dogs and cats are *big*," Dad said.

"Well, smaller then," said Iggy. "A rabbit or a guinea pig or – I know! – a *hamster*."

"What about an ant or a spider or an earwig?" Dad said. "They're small and they're very little trouble."

"*Ewww*," Iggy said. "I don't want them. I want something nice and soft and furry."

"Some spiders are furry," I said.

Iggy glared at me. "I don't want a *spider*, Flo," she said. "I want a *hamster*."

"Good luck with that," said Dad, and he went back to his reading.

"Put it on your birthday list," said Mum.

"What birthday list?"

"A list of things you'd like for your birthday,"

Mum said. "You could start making it now."

So Iggy did.

She went straightaway to get some pens and paper. She sat at the table in the garden, and she put pebbles on the corners to stop her list flapping around and blowing away. Then she tipped all the pens out of her pencil case and put on her very busy face.

At the top she wrote IGGY'S BIRTHDAY LIST in big, all-different-colour letters.

"Look Flo," she said, and she held it up for me to see.

"Cool," I said.

Then she put 1: A hamster

"Look, Flo," she said again.

"That's good."

Iggy sat and thought for a minute. "If I only put one thing on my list, will I definitely get it?"

"No," said Mum and Dad together.

"What will I get then?" Iggy said.

I said, "A surprise."

"I don't like surprises," said Iggy.

"Why not?"

"Because I don't know what they are."

28

Dad laughed.

"That's the whole point," I told her. "That's what surprises are."

Mum said, "Do you remember when you thought we were going to the supermarket and we went to the Safari Park instead? You were really surprised then."

"Oh yes," Iggy said. "I forgot. I do like surprises."

"Good," said Mum.

"But I like hamsters more," Iggy said. "Can my surprise be a hamster?"

"No!" said Mum and Dad.

Iggy looked at her list of one thing for a long time. Mum did more digging and Dad did more newspaper rustling, and I waited for the birds to come and eat their snacks.

"What shall number two be?" Iggy said.

Mum said, "There's no hurry," and Dad said, "What about a motorbike?"

Iggy frowned at him. "I'm not *allowed* a motorbike. I'm too young for one of those."

"You'll think of something," said Mum.

I said, "I bet there are *loads* of things you want."

"Oooh," said Iggy. "If I write loads of things on my list, will I get them all?"

"No," said Mum and Dad.

"So why am I writing them?"

"To give us an idea of what you want," Mum said.

"A hamster," Iggy said. "A hamster, a hamster, a *hamster*!"

"OK, enough," said Dad. "This conversation is going round in circles."

"Hamsters do that," Iggy said. "Gruffles, the hamster in our class, is going round in circles all the time."

Mum looked very carefully into the hole that she was making and Dad looked very carefully at the news. They didn't say anything.

Iggy worked on her list of one thing until lunchtime.

"Look Flo," she said.

Next to 1: **A hamster** there was a very good picture of a hamster in its cage. It was peeking through the bars with its twitchy nose and its little hands showing.

Underneath that, Iggy had written 2: **??????**
The question marks were all the colours of the rainbow.

"I don't know what else to *want*," she said.

I said I would help her.

For lunch we had omelettes and tomatoes and lettuce. Normally Iggy is a big fidget and a big chatterbox at the table, and she takes ages to finish. Today she was still and quiet and eating.

"Are you OK, Iggy?" Dad said. "You are acting very strangely."

"No I'm not," said Iggy. "I'm thinking."

"Thinking about what?" Mum said.

"What I want that isn't a hamster," Iggy said.

Mum and Dad laughed, and she frowned at them. She said, "It's harder than you think."

After lunch we started thinking together.

"What do other people have that you would like?" I said.

"Our whole class has a hamster."

"Apart from one of those," I said. "That's on the list already."

"Frankie Day's got a bike," Iggy said.

"What sort of bike?"

"A brilliant one. It's got tassels on the handlebars and a bell. It's got a basket for stuff at the front and a special seat for teddies at the back."

"Wow," I said. "What colour is it?"

"Pink and purple."

"What colour bike would you have if you could?"

"Pink and purple," Iggy said. "If I could, I'd

have one *exactly* the same."

"So write it down."

Next to 2: Iggy put **A bike like Frankie's**, and she drew it too, with tassels and a bear all strapped in behind the saddle.

When she had finished we both looked at it. "I'd really like one of those,' she said.

I said, "That's why it's number two on your list, because you'd really like it."

"So," Iggy said, "if I didn't really want something, it would be really later on in the list."

"Exactly," I said. "Like what?"

"Like poo on a stick, or to have to kiss a frog, or get tickled till I'm sick."

"Those could be really low down on your

list," I said. "Or you could just not put them there at all."

"What else?" she said. "What else do I want that other people have got?"

"I don't know," I said. I told her about my best friend Star. She's got a plug-in piano in her bedroom. I'd really like one.

"Noah Green has got a telly in his bedroom," Iggy said. "Shall I want one of those?"

"Don't bother," said Dad, walking past with his cup of coffee. "It will never happen."

Iggy screwed her face up with more thinking. "I know," she said. "I like Elsa Russell's shoes."

"What are they like?"

"They are red trainers with her own name on. She made them on the computer and they arrived in a box."

She put **3: Shoes with my name on**, and she drew them too. The way Iggy draws shoes is funny. They looked like big boats.

"What about clothes?" I said. "Would some new clothes be good?"

Iggy chewed her pencil. She wrote **4: A party dress for my party.**

Then without any help at all, Iggy wrote and drew

5: A treehouse with curtains

6: A trampoline

7: A doll with real hair you can cut and not get told off

8: A clock like Gabe Turner

"What sort of clock has Gabe got?" I said.

"It barks like a dog," Iggy said. "He brought it in for Show and Tell. It's funny."

"Ooh!" she said, and she wrote 9: Pants with days of the week on.

"Those," she said, "are actually quite useful."

"Let's think of one more," I said. "Then you've got ten things. That's a pretty good list."

"Easy," she said.

10: A hamster

"You already wrote that," I said.

I know," said Iggy. "But I especially, doubly want it."

She took the list to show Mum and Dad. They had swapped places. Mum was reading in the deck chair and Dad was digging.

"Very good," Dad said.

"Great pictures," said Mum.

"Where do I put it?" said Iggy.

"Somewhere it won't get lost," said Mum.

"Where's *that*?" Dad said. (Things are always getting lost in our house.)

"Put it on the fridge," I said. Mum puts

important pieces of paper there. "Put it on the fridge with a magnet."

Iggy ran off, flapping her list.

"What does she want then, Flo?" Dad said when Iggy was gone.

"She wants a hamster."

"She wants *two* hamsters," Mum said, "according to that list."

"And apart from two hamsters?" Dad said.

"She wants a bike," I said. "She wants a pink and purple bike with tassels on the handlebars, and a bell and a basket, and a seat for teddies."

Just then Iggy ran out with her list again. "I thought of another thing!"

"What is it?" I said.

"I need an ambulance."

"A what?"

"An ambulance for my toy hospital," she said.

11: Ambulance for teddies

And, "Oh!" she said.

12: Shelf for my books

And, "Oh yes!"

13: A pretend phone that looks really really real

And then, "Just one more..."

14: A HAMSTER

# Poor Iggy

When Mum and Dad woke me up in the morning I heard a strange sound. It was Iggy.

Iggy normally sings and chatterboxes when we are waking up, but today she was just groaning. It was quite loud.

"Can you hear that?" said Mum.

"Yes," I said. "Why's she doing that?"

"She's not very well, Flo," Mum said.

"Poor Iggy!" I said. "Not very well how?"

Mum said, "She's got a bad tummy. She's

been up all night. We've hardly slept a wink."

Before breakfast I went into Iggy's room to see her. She was a bit of a funny colour. "Are you all right?" I said.

"No," Iggy said, and she shivered even though she was under all her covers up to her chin.

"Are you cold?" I said.

"No," said Iggy, frowning at me. "I'm *boiling*." And then I had to get out of the way because she needed to go to the loo double quick.

All that day and the next, Iggy didn't do any smiling. She didn't want to play. Not even schools or shops or hospitals. She didn't want to eat anything, definitely not cake. She didn't want to read a book even, or watch anything on the telly.

She just stayed in her bed, and was all hot and cold, and went to the loo a lot.

At first it was peaceful.

You could draw a picture or do your homework or make a piece of toast, without anyone interrupting.

You could be on your own if you wanted, without anyone making a fuss.

You could start a game and play it until you

were finished, without anybody changing the rules.

At first it was fine, but after a while it didn't feel right. It was like a bit of Iggy had fallen out and she wasn't Iggy any more.

Dad missed her singing while she cleaned her teeth.

Mum missed her playing a tune every time she walked past the piano, even when she was supposed to be in a hurry.

I missed her talking at a million miles an hour and always making me laugh. I wanted Iggy to get better and come back. Mum and Dad agreed.

The next day Mum took Iggy to the doctor. The doctor gave her some pink medicine. He said she had to rest and stay off school and only eat a very little of what she fancied.

That night, Iggy still didn't fancy anything, except some sips of water. She went up the stairs very slowly like she was climbing a big mountain and she went straight to bed.

"Oh dear," Mum said. "She's not so good."

Dad shook his head.

"Poor Iggy!" I said.

In the morning, Iggy fancied rice crispies with sugar and no milk. Mum took it up to her room on a tray. We are *never* normally allowed rice crispies with sugar and no milk. We are *never, ever* normally allowed to eat in bed.

Iggy had two bowls.

I went up to say goodbye to her before school.

I said, "Is your tummy better?"

"No," said Iggy with her mouth full.

When I got home from school, Iggy wasn't in bed. She was tucked up on the sofa under a blanket. She had a drink and a yogurt and three biscuits all lined up on a little table beside her. She had the remote control for the TV in her hand. She was watching cartoons.

"I'm sick," she said with a really big grin on her face.

I put my school bags down and took off my shoes. "I know," I said.

"I had to just sit here, *all* day," she said, without taking her eyes off the telly.

"OK," I said.

"And I had to eat things that I like, and not eat things that I don't."

"Can I have a biscuit?" I said.

"Nope," said Iggy.

"Why not?" I asked.

"Germs," Iggy said. "You might catch them."

Just then Mum came in with a snack for me – a peanut butter sandwich and an apple and a glass of milk.

Iggy's voice went all wobbly and weak and feeble. "Can I have a sandwich?" she said.

"What do you want in it?" Mum said.

"Peanut butter and marmite and cheese," she said.

Mum and me said, "Together?" together.

"It's delicious," Iggy said, in her smallest, quietest, sickest voice.

"How's your tummy?" Mum said.

"Sore," Iggy said.

"Oh dear," said Mum.

But as soon as Mum left, Iggy munched on a biscuit.

When Dad came home the first thing he said was, "How's the patient?"

"Tired," Iggy said in her smallest sleepiest voice.

"Much better," said Mum.

"No I'm not," said Iggy.

"Well, you sit there," Dad said, "and me and Mum and Flo will look after you."

Iggy thought of a new thing we could get her about every three minutes. First it was her pencil case. Then it was a glass of milk. Then it

was her other pencil case and her sketchbook and her kangaroo and her nail varnish and a cut-up apple.

"Is it your tummy that's not working or your legs?" Dad said, and Iggy frowned at him.

"It's my tummy, silly," she said. "My legs are perfectly fine."

"Are you sure?" Dad said. "Have you checked?"

Iggy scowled at him while he had a peep under the blanket to see if her legs were still there. When she finished scowling, she clutched her tummy and groaned. "Owwwww!" she said, and, "Oaoooooh!"

She opened one eye to make sure we were watching while she did it.

"Oh dear," Dad said. "If you're *that* sick, you'd better go straight to bed."

Iggy stopped groaning straightaway. "I don't want to go to bed," she said.

"Yes you do," Dad said, and he whisked her up the stairs and tucked her in nicely.

When Dad came back he said, "So how are we going to make Iggy better?"

"She is better," Mum said.

"I know that," Dad said, "and you know that. But how do we make *Iggy* know she's better?"

I said, "I'm sure she'll get better in time for her birthday."

Mum and Dad looked at each other.

Mum said, "Of course she will."

Dad said, "Because if she's not better, her birthday will be *cancelled*."

"If Iggy is still sick," Mum said, "she'll have to stay in bed for the whole thing."

Dad winked at Mum. Then he said, "Flo, I think you should go and tell her."

So I went upstairs and into Iggy's room. She was drawing a picture and eating a biscuit. She hid it under the covers when I walked in.

I said, "I need to tell you something."

"What?" Iggy said. She brushed the biscuit crumbs off her covers and on to the floor.

"I think your birthday is going to get cancelled."

"What's cancelled?" Iggy said. She didn't look too worried.

"When something's cancelled," I said, "it means it doesn't happen."

Iggy stopped chewing. "Like Sports Day?" she said.

Our school had a Sports Day, but it rained and rained and rained. Instead of the egg and spoon race, and the mums and dads race, we did normal lessons. And there weren't any prizes.

"Like Sports Day," I said.

Iggy's chin wobbled and her eyes filled up with water. "Is that going to happen to my birthday?" she said.

"I don't know," I said. "Maybe, if you're sick. Dad said."

"Dad said?"

"Yep."

Iggy started to sniffle. "Does that mean I'll stay five?" she said. "I don't want to stay five."

"It doesn't mean you'll stay five," I said. "It just means you won't have a party and fun stuff."

"You have to have a party on your birthday," Iggy said. "You can't not have the fun stuff."

"I know," I said.

"I want the fun stuff!" Iggy said.

"Then you can't be sick any more," I said. "You have to get better."

"Is that all?" Iggy said.

I said, "I think so."

"OK," Iggy said. She got out from under her covers.

"What are you doing?" I said.

"I'm better," Iggy said.

"It's bedtime," I said. "You can get better in the morning."

"OK," Iggy said, and she got into bed.

"Good night," I said.

"Night, Flo," Iggy said.

In the morning, Iggy was up very early. My clock said something beginning with six which is *much* earlier than getting up time. I heard her walk into Mum and Dad's room. I heard her say, "I'm better."

"Good," Mum said.

"Great," said Dad.

"So don't Sports Day my birthday," Iggy said.

"What?" Mum said, and Dad said, "Am I still asleep?"

"I'm better, so I can be six and have a party and all the fun stuff," said Iggy. "OK?"

Dad laughed, and Mum said, "OK."

Iggy came into my room. I opened one eye. She was dressed in her school uniform.

"I'm better," she said.

"I know," I said. "I heard you."

"My birthday is back," she said.

"That's good. I'm glad."

"Will you wake up now?" she said.

"It's too early," I said.

"Mum and Dad are still in bed," she said.

I opened both eyes. "I've got a good idea," I said.

"What?" said Iggy.

"Let's go downstairs and eat rice crispies with sugar and no milk before they get up," I said.

So we did.

# Iggy and the Snow Queen

Iggy and me were making a play. We were learning our words and making our own costumes and scenery and everything. Our play was about the Snow Queen.

The Snow Queen is a lady who can turn you all to ice just by looking at you. She is very pretty with her coat and her gloves on, but underneath her fingers are made of icicles and her skin is as cold as a snowball. She pretends to be friendly and nice until she's got you where she wants you, and then she turns you into a snowman or an ice cube, just for fun. You wouldn't want to meet the Snow Queen in real life.

Iggy wanted to be the Snow Queen in our play for four reasons.

One, because she still fitted into the white furry coat in our dressing-up box and it was the perfect Snow Queen costume.

Two, because she'd been practising her mean face in the mirror. She screwed up her nose until it was all just wrinkles, and she bared all her snow-white teeth, and she stared at her reflection really hard like she was angry with it.

Three, because it was the starring role, the best part, and Iggy was interested in that.

Four, because it was nearly her birthday, and that was becoming Iggy's biggest reason for getting what she wanted.

I didn't mind.

We put flour on Iggy's face with cotton wool, and blue chalk on her lips and her cheeks, so she looked like she was actually frozen. The whites of her eyes looked warm and yellow against her skin. Her mouth was all pink on the inside when she smiled.

"Don't smile," I said.

"I'm not," Iggy said, and I saw pink when she talked too.

Underneath the white coat she wore a white nightie, white tights and white knickers and vest. We found some white gloves that were all lacy like the curtains at Granny and Grandpa's house. And we made a sort of crown out of tin foil and white pipe cleaners. That took ages.

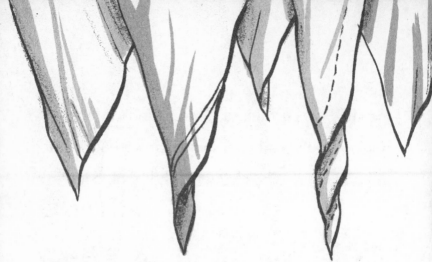

Then we made the scenery. We put all the white sheets and towels we could find on the floor of the landing and over the banisters. I climbed up and stuck some hankies and tea towels to the ceiling so they hung down like icicles.

"Cool," Iggy said.

"No Iggy," I said, and I pretended to shiver. "*Freezing.*"

We got all the white toys we had, like rabbits and polar bears and puppies and mice, and we dotted them about like frozen things. We put pillowcases over some of our other not-white teddies and they looked exactly like lumps of snow.

Dad came upstairs and looked at the landing. "What the…?" he said, in a quite loud voice.

"What is it?" Mum called from downstairs.

"The airing cupboard's exploded," he said.

"You're joking," Mum said and then she came up too. She opened her mouth and an "Ooh," came out.

"Not really," said Dad.

"What's going on?" they both said.

Iggy said, "It's the Snow Queen's lair," and she pulled her mean face.

I said we were doing a play.

"For you to watch," Iggy said.

One of the hankies on the ceiling was tickling Dad's head. "What's that about?" he said.

"They're *icicles*," Iggy told him.

"Silly me," Dad said, smiling at Mum. "I thought they were *handkerchiefs*."

Mum said a play sounded like a good idea as long as we promised to clear up afterwards. "Every single thing," she said.

"It's a very good lair," Dad said.

"Thanks," I said, and Iggy said, "We know."

In our play, I was a girl who got kidnapped by the Snow Queen and taken to her magic kingdom. I had to wear summer clothes because I was on a beach when it happened. Iggy put pink face-paint all over me so I looked sunburned. I had sunglasses and flip flops and a swimsuit and a towel.

"You are going to be *cold* when we get there," Iggy said.

"I know," I said, and I wrapped the towel around me like Mum does when she gets out of the bath. "I'm cold already."

"I'll kidnap you by being friendly and extra nice," Iggy said. "Then I'll turn you into a snowman!"

She threw a sheet over me and practised her best evil laugh. "Mwa ha ha!"

It sounded good from under my sheet.

"Then I can melt myself," I said, "and rescue all the other frozen things and change the Snow Queen's kingdom with my summery ways."

I covered some of the white sheets with colourful towels. "Look!" I said. "The snow is melting. And so will you, into a big puddle."

"Mwa ha ha!" Iggy laughed again, like she had other ideas.

We practised loads of times. When it was ready, we made tickets with Mum and Dad's names on. Iggy wanted them to buy the tickets for 50p, but Dad just tickled her until she stopped asking.

They had a cushion each to sit on at the edge of the Snow Queen's lair.

"This is really good," said Mum, smiling.

Then I turned all the lights off and the play began.

Iggy was supposed to start with her evil laugh. She was supposed to put pillowcases over my blue rabbit and her orange kangaroo, like she was turning them to ice. She was supposed to say, "Everything is lovely and *cold*."

Instead, she stood there grinning at Mum and Dad, showing the pink inside of her mouth.

"*Iggy*," I whispered. "*Do your laugh*."

"Oh," Iggy said. "Heeheehee."

It didn't sound evil at all.

"*Iggy*," I whispered. "*Turn the teddies to ice.*"

"Oh," Iggy said. "Where are the pillow things?"

"*Say the line, Iggy*," I whispered.

"I can't remember it," she said. "Stop whispering at me."

"Oh dear," Dad said.

Mum said, "Do you need more time to practise?"

Iggy didn't answer. She just stood there, grinning at them. It was like the real Snow Queen had turned her to ice right there on the landing.

"We've practised *loads*," I said.

Nobody said anything. I counted to ten in my head, and then I counted again.

"Shall we come back later?" Dad said.

"Mwah ha ha!" Iggy said suddenly. It made us all jump. She was pulling her mean face *perfectly*.

"Oh, are we back on?" said Mum.

"I don't like the look of her," Dad said, pointing at the Snow Queen.

"Mwah ha ha!" Iggy said again, even better.

"I'm *scared*," Dad said.

"Stop it, Dad," I said.

And Iggy went up really close to him and hissed, "Or I'll turn you to *ice*!"

She wasn't supposed to say that. We hadn't practised it or anything, but it was really good.

In the end, Iggy said a lot of things she wasn't supposed to. I didn't mind. I added a few things too.

The play was much longer than we meant it to be. Mum and Dad asked for an interval so they could put the supper on. And they really clapped at the end. They stood up and everything. Dad said that was called a "standing ovation".

He said, "Not every actor gets one of those, you know."

Later, after we cleaned up (which took ages) and had our supper and washed our make-up off in the bath and cleaned our teeth and had books, Iggy came into my room.

She said, "That was the best game ever. I'm going to be the Snow Queen when I grow up."

"You don't have to be the Snow Queen every time," I said. "We could do another play."

"A different one?" said Iggy.

"We could do Hansel and Gretel."

"Can I be the wicked stepmother?"

"We could do Little Red Riding Hood."

"I want to be the wolf."

"Let's do one tomorrow," I said, and Iggy jumped around in my room with excitement.

"Get into bed!" Dad shouted up the stairs.

"Mwa ha ha!" Iggy whispered to me, then she skipped down the landing to her own room.

# Iggy and the birthday cakes

Because it was going to be Iggy's birthday we were making cakes for her to take to school. She wanted one fairy cake for everyone in her class.

"That's thirty cakes," Mum said.

"Thirty-one," Iggy said. "There's a new boy."

"I don't know how you move in that classroom," Mum said.

"We don't," said Iggy. "We're not allowed.

We have to sit still nearly all the time."

"What sort of thirty-one cakes do you want?"
Mum said.

Iggy said she wanted little ones, all covered
with sweets and sprinkles and icing

"Can I help?" I said. I like making cakes.

"I'm counting on it," Mum said. Iggy jumped
up and down on the spot and I smiled.

I like cooking of all kinds. Iggy likes cooking
too. She likes it because of the eating. Mum says
if you're cooking with Iggy, you have to watch
her like a hawk. If you take your eyes off her for
even a minute, things disappear before they get
cooked.

We went to the shop to buy the things we
needed.

To make a cake you need eggs, sugar, butter and flour and a magic thing called baking powder that fills the cakes with air when you're not looking. To make thirty-one cakes you need a lot of all those things.

To make icing you need icing sugar and water, but only a drop.

To decorate a cake you need chocolate buttons, chocolate sprinkles, rainbow sprinkles, silver balls, dolly mixtures and Smarties. You also need special icing that comes in a tube like a tiny toothpaste, in four different colours, that you can actually draw a picture with.

That's what you need.

Mum said we could choose two things each and two things only. Iggy chose Smarties and silver balls. I picked rainbow sprinkles and special icing.

I said, "These are going to be the best cakes ever."

Mum said, "I agree."

Iggy said nothing because she had Smarties in her mouth.

"Give those to me, madam," Mum said.

I think Iggy said, "Sorry," but she did it with her mouth closed so we couldn't count how many she was eating.

When we got home we put all the things we'd bought on the kitchen counter. Mum got the stepladder for Iggy because she's a little bit little to see what she is stirring.

First we had to wash our hands. Mum said this was very important because nobody in Iggy's class wanted to eat a cake that gave them a tummy bug.

"I know," Iggy said. "Cakes are supposed to be more fun than that."

We put the sugar and the butter in a big bowl on the scales. I did the butter and Iggy did the sugar. We had to get just the right amounts of them, which meant watching the numbers and shouting, "Stop!" when they got to 4. Iggy was so busy looking at the numbers that she sort of missed the bowl. Sugar started pouring off the edge of the table.

"Stop!" said Mum.

"It's only on 3," said Iggy.

"There's three more on the floor," Mum said, getting the dustpan and brush.

"Oops," said Iggy. "Never mind."

We mixed the butter and sugar together until they went all creamy and fluffy. My arm ached after about six stirs and I had to have a rest. Iggy's ached even quicker, but Mum is very strong and her arm hardly ached at all. We took it in turns.

"There," Mum said. "That'll do."

Iggy put her finger in and scooped a blob into her mouth. "That's not nice," she said, pulling a face.

"Don't eat it then," Mum said, and she made Iggy wash her hands again.

After that we put the flour and the eggs and the magic powder in. We had to crack the eggs without getting bits of shell and gloop everywhere. It wasn't easy.

Iggy didn't like the feel of egg white on her hands. "Yeuch," she said, and she washed her hands without even being asked.

Mum got out the special cake tray with the round holes and Iggy put the paper cases in. There were twelve holes in the tray. Iggy counted them.

"That's not enough," she said.

"I know," Mum said.

"There has to be thirty-one," Iggy said.

Mum said they didn't make a tray with thirty one holes in. She said, "We've only got this one with twelve holes in. Which means we are going to have to do this three times."

"That makes thirty-six," I said, because I'm learning my twelve times table. "Three times twelve is thirty-six."

Mum scruffed my hair up at the top. "Maths Whizz," she said.

"That's too many," Iggy said.

"You can give one to your teacher," I said.

"And your dad will eat four," Mum said.

Iggy frowned. "No he *won't*," she said.

We put spoonfuls of cake mix into the paper cases. They didn't look like much splodged in the bottom, but Mum said once they started cooking they'd fill up to the top with cake.

The bowl was still full of cake mix. Every time Mum wasn't looking, Iggy stuck her finger in and ate some.

"You're going to make yourself sick," Mum said, without even seeing.

"How do you know?" Iggy said. She wiped her finger on her T-shirt and made her face all still, like when she's hiding something.

"Because I know *you*," Mum said, tickling her. "And I know how yummy cake mix is too."

Iggy grinned and licked her lips.

Mum put the splodges in the oven. We had to wait twelve whole minutes until they were done. It felt like forever.

When the first twelve came out, Mum said we had to leave them to cool or the icing would just dribble off. She said, "Icing doesn't like getting hot."

We put twelve more splodges in the oven.

While we were waiting and waiting, Mum put two bowls on the table. She put the Smarties in one and the silver balls in another. The rainbow sprinkles had their own pot with a sprinkly hole to pour them through. I laid out

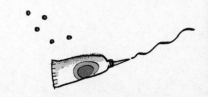

the special icing tubes in a neat row of yellow, green, red and black.

Every time I looked away from Iggy I heard a crunching noise. "What are you eating?" I said.

"Nothing," Iggy said, but she had bits of Smartie on her teeth, I could see.

"Mum," I said, "she's eating the smarties."

"Hands off, Iggy," Mum said. "Just wait. It won't be long."

I looked at Mum, and when I did I heard more chewing.

"Iggy!" I said, and Iggy said, "What?"

She was smiling and her smile was full of rainbows.

"Stop *eating* stuff," I said.

"I'm *not*," she said, with sprinkle juice

squeezing from the corners of her lips.

Mum said, "Let's make the icing."

We put the icing sugar in a bowl and then we dripped a drip of water in, and Iggy stirred. It took three drips to turn a whole lot of sugar into icing.

When I said to Mum, "That's amazing," I heard a slurping noise.

Iggy had icing on her fingers and she was licking it off.

"How did you get icing on your fingers?" Mum said.

Iggy shrugged and slurped some more. "I slipped," she said.

"Fingers *out*," said Mum. "I mean it."

I looked at Mum and I heard a rattling sound, like tiny marbles. "What's that?" I said.

"I don't know," said Iggy, with a mouth full of silver balls.

"No more," Mum said. "That's enough. You'll have nothing left for your cakes."

I could see Iggy looking at the special icing in the tubes. I knew what she was thinking. I've seen her eat toothpaste out of the tube before. On holiday she ate toothpaste until she was sick.

Iggy's hand reached out for the red icing. She had a gleam in her eye.

"Mum! Help!" I said, and I crashed my hand down on the table to stop her. "She's going to eat the special icing!"

Mum said we both had to leave and do something else for ten minutes. She said, "Out, both of you. Go and draw a design of what your cakes will look like."

So we did. I drew the crinkly paper cups, and I used red and yellow and green and black pens for the special icing. My cakes had cats and dogs and faces and flowers on.

Iggy used all her pencils for the rainbow sprinkles. "Delicious," she said, and she pretended to eat her own picture.

"You're a greedy pig," I said. Iggy snorted just like one and we fell about laughing.

"What's so funny?" Mum said with her head around the door.

"Oink oink," said Iggy, and we fell about laughing some more.

"Cakes are ready," Mum said. We got up and raced to the kitchen in no time flat.

Mum was right. The paper cases were filled to the top with bubbly cake. The air smelled like hot butter. My mouth was watering.

We had six cakes each to play with.

The white icing wasn't too runny and it wasn't too hard. It was just right. I dangled it from my spoon and it sat on top of the cake in an almost-circle.

"Perfect," Mum said.

Iggy swirled her spoon and the icing landed on her cake in crazy squiggles.

"Perfect," said Iggy.

I drew a cat with the special black icing. It sort of looked like one. I gave it silver balls for eyes and rainbow sprinkle whiskers.

"Brilliant," said Mum.

Iggy squidged one black blob on her squiggly icing and one black blob straight in her mouth. She popped a Smartie in the middle.

"Brilliant," Iggy said.

I put my first cake on a plate to dry. "Next one," I said.

Iggy tore her paper case off and took a big bite. "Next one," Iggy said, spraying crumbs.

This time I did another almost-circle and a red flower with a green leaf. I put silver balls all round the outside.

Iggy did more squiggling and squidging and popping.

On the third cake I did squiggling and squidging and popping too because it looked like fun.

 Iggy did a black and yellow bumblebee with Smarties for eyes.

"That is so good," I said.

"I know," Iggy told me.

We did all our cakes really well. We did heart cakes and crown cakes and star cakes and covered-in-everything cakes. Then we left them to dry and we helped Mum clean up. I cleaned up with a cloth and Iggy cleaned up with her eating. She emptied all the leftover sprinkles and silver balls and Smarties into her mouth and crunched them up.

She said, "What do we do with the special icing?"

"We don't eat it," Mum said, taking the little tubes away. "We'll be sick."

"No we won't," said Iggy. "We love icing."

"You can't eat icing on its own," Mum said.

"Why not?" said Iggy. "It's the best bit."

"Can we have a cake now, Mum?" I asked. It was hard looking at them all sitting there. It was hard to look at them and not have one.

"Just one," Mum said.

I picked a flower cake and Iggy picked an everything cake.

"Do you want one, Mum?" Iggy said.

"I don't mind if I do," Mum said, and she picked a star one.

"Well," Iggy said, "if you're having another one then so can we," and she grabbed one and put her teeth in it before anyone could argue. I think it was her bee one.

"Iggy!" Mum said. "That's your third cake!"

"It's yummy," said Iggy, nodding.

After that I did my homework, which was money. Mum was on the phone to her sister, my Auntie Kate, who lives in America. Neither of us was watching Iggy like a hawk.

When Dad came home from work and I went to show him the cakes, there were only eight left.

Mum was cross. She said Iggy couldn't take eight cakes in to school for thirty-one children. She said, "Eight cakes is worse than no cakes at all."

"Where's that Piggy Iggy?" Dad said.

We found her on the sofa. She was frowning at the TV and she was holding her tummy. She was a bit green.

"I don't feel sick at all," she said. "It's not the cakes. It wasn't me."

Dad got her a drink of water.

I said to Mum, "Are you going to make more cakes tomorrow, for Iggy's class?" and Mum said, "Yes."

"Good," said Dad, and he winked at me. "That means I can eat one. Do you want one, Iggy?"

"No," Iggy groaned. "I don't like cake."

"Yes you do," Dad said. "You love cake."

"Not today I don't," Iggy told him.

Dad said, "Will you like cake tomorrow?"

"Don't know," Iggy said. "Maybe. Probably."

So Dad said we'd save her one to put in her lunchbox.

And the next day when we made the new cakes, we didn't have to watch Iggy one bit.

# Happy birthday, Iggy!

Iggy woke up very, *very* early on her birthday. It was still dark and the birds weren't singing. She ran around upstairs in the house, giggling. She burst into my room, and then ran out again and burst into Mum and Dad's.

"Wake up, wake up, WAKE UP!!!!" she shouted. "It's my BIRTHDAY!"

Mum said, "Happy birthday, darling."

Dad said, "Even the birds are still asleep."

I got out of bed and went to join in. I love birthdays, and Iggy's birthday is the best one after mine because she gets so excited you think she might pop.

Dad was lying on his tummy with his pillow over his head and Mum's hair was all funny. Iggy was screwed up into the tightest, most excited ball in between them on the bed. Her face was all screwed up too and her nose was all wrinkly, and her smile was the biggest, widest thing about her.

"*Birthday*!" she squeaked.

"*I know*!" I squeaked back.

"*Exciting*!" she squeaked.

"Sleeping," Dad said.

"Not any more," said Mum.

"Coffee," Dad said.

So Mum and Iggy and me went to make Dad some coffee.

Downstairs in the kitchen it was *definitely* Iggy's birthday. There was a pile of presents on the table, and a heap of cards. There was a piece of string hanging near the ceiling with bits of paper pegged on that said HAPPY BIRTHDAY

all across the room. Each letter was as big as a page and coloured in with hearts and stars and dots and things.

"*Wow!*" popped Iggy.

"Cool," I said.

"You like?" said Mum. She was wearing her dressing gown that Dad says makes her look like a monk. She looked really sleepy.

"*Wow!*" popped Iggy again.

The light in the kitchen looked really bright because of the dark outside. I felt like we were on the inside of a TV.

"Nobody else is awake," Mum said into the sink.

Iggy was dancing around the kitchen. She was twirling and flipping, and her nightie made a circle around her and her feet went shuffle shuffle on the floor.

"Can she open a present?" I said to Mum.

"*Ooh, present*," Iggy said, and she stopped twirling.

There were six presents on the table. They were wrapped up in paper with spots and birds and stars and funny stick people on. The one with the funny stick people on it was from me.

"Can she open mine?" I said.

"*Yesyesyesyes!*" said Iggy. She held her hands out for it. I took it off the pile and gave it to her.

"Happy birthday, Iggy," I said.

Suddenly Iggy looked very serious and important. "Thank you, Flo," she said, and she stared at the paper and gave my present a squeeze.

"Let's go and open it with Dad," Mum said. She carried two cups of coffee up the stairs in front of us.

Iggy was next, carrying her present very carefully, like there might be a living creature inside. We all knew Iggy had been hoping for a puppy or a kitten or a guinea pig or a hamster. Especially a hamster.

My present for Iggy wasn't any of those. It was a pencil case. A blue pencil case with rainbows and aliens all over it. It was the nicest pencil case I had ever seen. I was really hoping that Iggy was going to think so too.

She squeezed it again on the way up the stairs. She didn't know it was a pencil case yet. For a living creature it was keeping very, very still.

Dad was sleeping again. Iggy and me woke him up with bouncing. He groaned.

"Come *on*, Dad," Iggy said. "I've got *presents*."

Dad sat up. "Ooh," he said in his best little girl voice. "I *love* presents."

Iggy made sure we were all looking and then she started to unwrap her present s-l-o-w-l-y, peeling off the sticky tape and smoothing out the creases in the paper.

"Can I have another nap while you do that?" said Dad.

"Sssh!" said Iggy. "No!"

Iggy liked her pencil case. She gave me a big hug and a kiss, and we were a bit bouncy again. Dad spilled his coffee.

"Oops," Iggy said, smiling at him. "Sorry."

After her pencil case, Iggy concentrated on her breathing and didn't say anything.

"What's up?" Mum said.

"Nothing," said Iggy. "I'm trying not to open another present until after breakfast."

"OK," said Mum.

"Can we have breakfast now?" said Iggy.

Iggy's birthday breakfast was hot chocolate and little pancakes with banana and syrup. We ate it while the sun was coming up. The light through the kitchen window was all pink.

"When's my party?" Iggy said with a mouth full of pancake.

"It's after lunch," Mum said.

"What?" Iggy said. She looked horrified. "That's ages! Can we have lunch now?"

"You're still eating your breakfast, silly," said Mum. "Why don't you open another present?"

Iggy opened her whole pile of presents at the table. She got a jigsaw puzzle map of the world, a dress to wear to her party, a first-aid kit for her toy hospital, a book token for £10 and a game of Scrabble.

"Thank you," said Iggy, and "Wow!" and "Cool!" and "I've *always* wanted one of those."

When Mum and Dad got up to clear the table, Iggy and Me went upstairs to do her puzzle and bandage her teddies and try on her dress and look at her book token and play Scrabble, all at the same time. It didn't feel like very long at all before Mum called us to say that lunch was ready.

She and Dad had been hard at work. Downstairs looked like a party was about to happen. The table had a cloth on it, and there were red paper plates and purple paper cups and party hats and streamers and balloons *everywhere*.

"How did you do that?" Iggy said, her eyes all over the place.

While we ate lunch we could see the

sandwiches for the party, and the crisps and grapes and strawberries and sausage rolls and little cakes. We weren't allowed to touch those.

"Everyone will be here in an hour," said Mum.

Just then the doorbell rang.

"Somebody's here now," I said, and Mum and Dad smiled.

Iggy jumped up to open the door. It was Granny and Grandpa. Granny was at the door and Grandpa was getting something out of the back of their car.

"Happy birthday!" said Granny, and she gave Iggy a big hug.

"Thank you," said Iggy, with her eyes on Grandpa. "What you doing?" she said.

"Secret," he said. "Close your eyes."

Iggy did, but not for very long. "What have you got?" she said, with one eye open.

"I don't know," said Grandpa. "Why don't you come outside and see?"

We all went out to the car, Iggy, Mum, Dad, Granny and me. Grandpa had got the thing out and put it on the pavement. It was big and covered in a bin bag. I guessed what it was straightaway.

"Is it for me?" Iggy said.

"Yes," Mum said. "Have a look."

Iggy lifted a bit of the bin bag and had a peep. "*Ooooh!*" she said, like all the air was coming out of her at once, and she ripped the bin bag off in a big hurry.

It was a bike. A blue and pink and yellow and silver bike, with tassels on the handlebars and a bell and a special seat for teddies at the back.

"*Ooooh!*" Iggy said again, just staring and staring. She covered her eyes with her hands and then she looked again, to make sure it was still there.

"Happy birthday, Iggy!" said Granny and Grandpa.

Iggy and me and Granny and Grandpa went

for a bike ride around the block. We walked and
Iggy wobbled.

"This is the best birthday ever," she said.

When we got back, it was only ten minutes until the party started. Iggy and me put on our party hats and waited by the door. Dad tied two balloons to the gate so everyone would know which house to come to.

Iggy was allowed six of her friends from school. Everyone arrived at once. They all brought presents and they all talked at a million miles an hour, like Iggy.

It was brilliant. We played Pass the Parcel and Musical Bumps and Musical Statues and Sleeping Lions. Sleeping Lions is when everybody has to pretend to be asleep, and if you move or make a sound you're out. The last person to move is the winner. It is Dad's favourite party game for children.

Iggy won Sleeping Lions. She was the best by far. She didn't move a muscle or make a peep. One by one her friends got caught moving, or opening their eyes, or saying something. I was out just before Iggy.

"You're the winner, Iggy," Dad said.

She didn't move.

"Iggy," said Mum, "You've won! Come and get your prize."

Iggy didn't even open her eyes. Her face was all squished against the carpet and her hands were tucked up under her chest. Suddenly she let out a soft little snore. Iggy was fast asleep.

Mum tried to wake her up, but Iggy stayed asleep. It was no good. Nobody could wake her.

The mums and dads came for Iggy's friends. They whispered goodbye to Iggy and took their party bags home.

Iggy carried on sleeping.

When everyone had gone and the party was all tidied away, Iggy was still asleep. Dad carried her upstairs with me and mum following behind. He put Iggy to bed in her party dress. She didn't wake up.

"Happy birthday, Iggy!" we whispered, and Mum turned out the light.

# Iggy on wheels

After Iggy's birthday, a big parcel arrived at the door. It wouldn't fit through the letterbox because it was too big. It was very exciting.

"What can it be?" Dad said, and Mum said, "Who's it for?"

Dad read the name on the front and then he frowned. "That's funny," he said.

"What?" Iggy and me and Mum said at the same time.

Dad scratched his head and looked at the

parcel again. "FLO AND IGGY" he said. "We don't know anyone with that name, do we?"

I said, "Silly!" and Iggy said, "GIVE IT!"

Dad put the parcel on the kitchen table and we crowded round.

Mum said, "It's from Kate."

Kate is our auntie. She is Mum's sister. She lives in America.

"What's she sending you stuff for?" Dad said. "It's not your birthday again, is it, Iggy? It's not yours now, is it, Flo? Did we forget? Are we terrible parents?"

We started ripping at the brown paper.

"Like wild animals," Dad said, and he tickled us while we were trying to rip.

Inside the brown paper were two shoeboxes

all done up with tape. On top of the shoeboxes was a card with a picture of a granny on a skateboard. She was wearing a flowery skirt and a cardigan and glasses, just like our Granny does. The hedges behind her were all blurred like she was going really fast. It looked funny.

Mum turned the card over. It said,

> *Dear Flo and Igs,*
> *I saw these in a sale*
> *and I thought of you. Don't*
> *let Mum and Dad borrow*
> *them.*
>
> *Kate xxx*

Mum got the scissors and cut the tape for us.

We opened our boxes. Inside were shoes. Black
and pink trainers with big pink laces.

"Cool!" Iggy said.

I took a trainer out of the box. "Why are they
so heavy?" I said, and I turned the shoe over in
my hands to see what it was made of.

Mum's mouth dropped open
and Dad put his hands over
his eyes. I laughed. The
trainers had wheels in
the bottom.

"COOL!" said Iggy.

Iggy and me kicked our ordinary shoes off
right there and left them where they fell, even
though Dad is *always* telling us not to do that.
He says that his worst thing to do at night is trip

over girls' shoes in the dark. He looks at Mum and says, "I am talking to *you* too."

We put on our new black and pink trainers with wheels and we stared at our feet in amazement. They didn't look like ordinary shoes. They didn't feel like ordinary shoes either. They had a life of their own. They were more like magic shoes that might take you wherever they wanted, any minute, without you even asking. I have always dreamt of having some of those.

"Wow!" I said.

"Wow!" Iggy said, like an echo.

I felt myself moving. I grabbed hold of Mum so I didn't roll away. Iggy grabbed hold of Dad.

"Wow!" said Mum and Dad.

The floor in our kitchen is made of big black tiles. Mum says they are very good at not showing the dirt, and Dad says they are very cold when you come down in the morning with no slippers on to make the coffee.

I say that they are very hard when you fall over on your bottom because your shoes have wheels in. Iggy and me fell over on the hard floor a lot. Shoes with wheels in take some getting used to.

After a bit, Mum and Dad stopped letting us hold on to them because they had other things to do.

Mum said, "I've got to get some work done."

Dad said, "I have to make Auntie Kate a thank you card."

Iggy and me made a route across the kitchen with places to grab on to. We went from the table,

to the fridge,

to the cupboard with the cereal in it,

to the sink.

From the table to the fridge was the longest. That's where we had the most falls. But we kept practising. We practised for ages.

Instead of saying, "Aaaah!" we started saying, "Wheeeeee!" And we started going from the table straight to the cereal cupboard, without even stopping at the fridge.

"Did you see *that?*" we said to Mum and Dad.

Sometimes they did and sometimes they didn't. And sometimes our feet rolled out from underneath us with no warning or anything, and we said, "Did you see *that?*" from down on the floor.

We didn't get bored, not even once.

Later that night we phoned Auntie Kate to say thank you.

Iggy said, "They are the best shoes ever."

Auntie Kate said, "I *know*. I just couldn't resist them. I wish they made them for grown-ups."

"We'll be really good at them next time you come to visit," I said. "We'll come and meet you at the airport on wheels."

"Ooh," said Auntie Kate. "The floor at the

airport would be *perfect*."

"How perfect?" Iggy said. "Why?"

"All smooth and shiny and no bumps," Kate said. "And BIG, so you can skate for miles!"

"When are you coming?" Iggy and me said together, at exactly the same time.

"Not for a while," she said. "But keep practising. And be on the lookout for good floors from now on."

After that, even though we weren't allowed outside yet with wheels on, Iggy and me became *experts* at floors. Everywhere we went, we imagined what they might be like to skate on, and every day we told each other what we found.

"Pavements would be tricky," I said. "Too many cracks."

"The school hall would be fun," Iggy said. "Imagine wheeling around in assembly."

"The playground would be juddery," I said.

"The playground is *sharp*," she said. "We'd have holes in our knees."

"The supermarket would be good," I said. "They've got smooth floors."

"True," said Iggy.

"And trolleys to hold on to," I said. "Supermarkets would be the best."

"Supermarkets. I know," said Iggy.

But we were wrong.

On Saturday Mum and Dad said we were going to see some art.

"What sort of art?" I said, and Iggy said, "I don't like it."

"What don't you like?" Mum said.

Iggy said, "Art. I don't want to."

Dad laughed. He said, "How come you spend half your time drawing if you don't like art?"

"I like *drawing it*," Iggy said. "I don't like *looking at it*."

"Well, we do," Mum said. "So let's go."

"Can we wear our wheels?" Iggy said.

Mum and Dad looked at each other. Mum's look said, "No way," and Dad's look said, "Oh, go on, let them."

So they did.

We were right about pavements. They were tricky. The wheels made a clickety sound over all the joins and sometimes it was hard to roll anywhere. We had to pick up our heavy feet and walk. On the bus my legs kept rolling away from me when we turned corners. It felt funny.

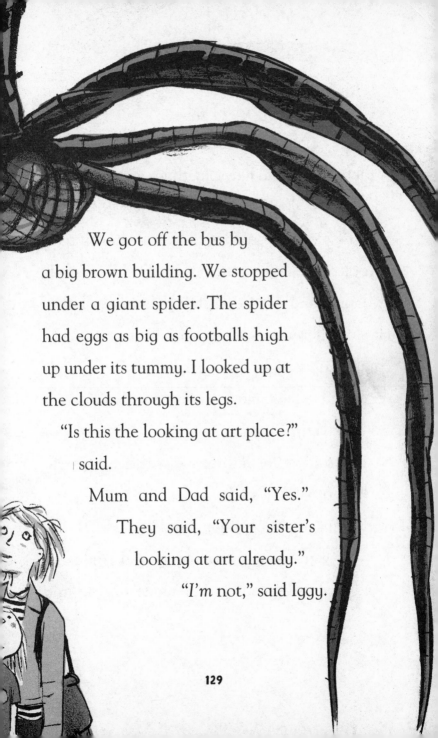

We got off the bus by
a big brown building. We stopped
under a giant spider. The spider
had eggs as big as footballs high
up under its tummy. I looked up at
the clouds through its legs.

"Is this the looking at art place?"
I said.

Mum and Dad said, "Yes."
They said, "Your sister's
looking at art already."

"*I'm* not," said Iggy.

"Suit yourself," said Dad.

"No," Iggy said. "I mean…" and she suddenly grabbed my hand like something important had happened. "I'm looking at the FLOOR."

The doors were opening and shutting as people were coming in and out. The floor inside was grey and shiny and enormous and A HILL. It sloped down all smooth, and the ceiling got higher and higher, and then it went flat. It could have been made for shoes with wheels.

"Heaven," Iggy said.

Dad said he could think of another word for it.

"What is it?" I said.

Mum said, "Never you mind."

We went through the doors and Dad said, "OK, let's see what you're made of. Me and

Mum will go and stand at the bottom."

"Are you sure about that?" Mum said.

"Will you catch us?" I said.

Dad said, "If we have to."

Mum said, "Don't go too fast."

I wasn't sure how to do that.

Iggy and me stood at the top of the slope and watched Mum and Dad walk down it. They got quite far away. There were people *everywhere*. I wasn't sure how not to bump into them.

"Do you think this is a good idea?" I said to Iggy.

Iggy didn't look at me. She was looking at Mum and Dad, way down at the bottom of the slope. She said. "Do you want to go first?"

"I don't know," I said.

"This is going to be really fast," she said.

I asked her if she was scared.

"*No*," Iggy said, but I think she was lying.

Neither of us moved.  Mum and Dad were pretending to fall asleep. Dad put his hands under his cheek like a pillow and shut his eyes. Mum acted like her knees weren't working.

"Will we be all right?" Iggy said.

"I think so," I said.

"Shall we count to three?" Iggy said.

"OK," I said. "One… Two…"

"Will you hold my hand?" she said.

I took Iggy's hand. It was all warm and fidgety. I took a deep breath.

"THREE!"

We were fast.

"Wheeeee!" we said.

We were so fast that we were at the bottom before we knew it and we could hardly remember how we got there. We didn't fall over. And we didn't bump into anybody. And we didn't let go of each other's hands.

"Again! Again!" Iggy shouted as soon as we stopped.

"I don't think so," said Mum.

"Why not?" I said.

"We *have* to!" Iggy said. She was holding on to Dad and wheeling around in circles.

"I think you're in trouble," Dad said, and we turned to see where he was looking.

A lady in a black uniform was walking down the hill towards us. She was looking at our feet and she didn't look happy. Iggy stopped wheeling. She stopped blinking even.

"Is she the *police?*" Iggy said. Her cheeks got very pink.

I held Mum's hand. "It's all right," she said. "Don't worry."

But not worrying was very hard.

The lady in the black uniform walked right up to where we were standing.  She looked down at us and I looked up at her. Iggy wouldn't look. She had her eyes closed.

"You mustn't do that," the lady said.

I nodded.

"You'll have to take the wheels out while you're here," she said, and Dad said, "OK."

"Sorry," Mum said.

Then the lady in the black uniform smiled. "It's OK," she said.

Iggy opened one eye to see if she had gone yet.

"You're very good at it," the lady said as she walked away. "You went very fast."

Iggy opened both her eyes. Her feet slid around a bit underneath her, but she didn't look pink or scared any more.

"That," Iggy said to me, "was the best floor *ever*."

# Iggy and the hamster

When Iggy went to school after her birthday, her teacher Rwaida asked her what her best present was.

"My bike," Iggy said. "*Definitely*."

"Ooh, you lucky girl," Rwaida said. "A bicycle is a lovely present to have."

"Yes," said Iggy, "but really I wanted a hamster."

Rwaida told Mum about it when we were collecting Iggy from her class. "The thing is," Rwaida said, "we do need someone to take care of Gruffles over half term. Perhaps Iggy would like to do it."

Half term is a bit in the middle of school where you don't have to go just in case you're getting tired of it. It is for a whole week. That means Iggy and me would have a hamster to look after for seven whole days.

"Please can we, Mum?" we said. "Please can we? *Please?*"

"I'm not sure," said Mum on the walk home.

"No way," said Dad when we asked him.

"Not on your Nelly,' he said when we asked him again.

"But…" we said.

"But nothing," said Dad.

"But they would really love it," I heard Mum saying to him in the kitchen. "And it's only a borrow. It's not actually theirs. We can give it back in a week."

"OK," said Dad.

"OK," said Mum. "You can look after the school hamster for half term."

Iggy did a little hamster dance around the sitting room, with her paws up by her cheeks and her teeth sticking out. She looked exactly like one. It gave everyone the giggles.

On Friday it was time to take Gruffles to our house. We watched him through the bars of his cage in the classroom. He was sleeping in his yellow house, all curled up into a little ball with his nose in his bottom. He was breathing really fast and his eyes were very shut.

"He's always doing that," said Iggy.

"What?" I said.

"Sleeping. He sleeps all day at school and we get told off when we try and wake him up."

"That's because he's nocturnal," Mum said.

Nocturnal is when you like to be awake at night and asleep in the morning.

"A bit like Dad," Iggy said.

"Yes, sometimes," said Mum.

Gruffles was the nicest hamster ever. He was a sort of peachy brown with a white splodge on his back and a smaller white splodge on his head. His nose was the smallest, pinkest, twitchiest nose I have ever seen. His eyes were like tiny ink drops, watery black.

"He can't see very well," Mum said.

"How do you know," said Iggy, waving at him.

"Because I know. Hamsters have bad eyesight, but they're very good at smelling and listening."

"OK," said Iggy, and she whispered to Gruffles, "I'll show you my special pens later. They smell of toothpaste and bubble gum and sun cream. You'll like them."

We put Gruffles's cage on the landing between mine and Iggy's rooms. Iggy wanted him in her room ("Because he's *my* class hamster") but Mum said it was out of the question. "He'll keep you awake at night with all his scuttling about,' she said.

"And your room will smell of wee," said Dad.

"*Ewww!*" said Iggy. "Gross!"

"And poo," Dad said, and she stuck her tongue out at him.

It was really fun having Gruffles. It was all Iggy and me wanted to do. Mum and Dad kept asking us if we wanted to go swimming, or shopping, or have a friend round for tea, but we didn't.

Every night we listened to him rattling along

on his little wheel and digging about in his sawdust.

Every morning we woke up extra early and we got the cage and took it into one of our rooms. We shut the door and sat in front of each other with our legs stretched out and our feet touching, and we took Gruffles out and put him in the middle between us. Our legs made a kind of a wall that he couldn't get over in a hurry. Then we took it in turns to pick him up and give him a cuddle. He was soft and blinking and trembly.

"I *love* him," Iggy said. "I just love love *love* him," and she gave him a tiny kiss on his tiny nose.

Gruffles did scuttling about and sniffing and twitching. His whiskers were always moving and his feet were tiny and naily and sharp. He was perfect in every way.

We didn't want to think about giving him back.

On the last day of half term, I got up and went to Gruffles's cage. It was Iggy's turn to have him in her room. I was yawning and stretching and walking, and then I stopped dead still in the middle of the landing because I'd just seen something that wasn't right.

The door to Gruffles's cage was open.

I said his name, "Gruffles?" just in case he was

there and he would hear me.

I peeked into his house. There was lots of ripped up tissue and sawdust and droppings, but there wasn't a ball of curled up breathing hamster.

"Oh no," I said.

Just then, Iggy came out of her room. "What?" she said.

I told her. "Gruffles is *gone!*"

Iggy gasped and we both looked around the floor for a scuttling hamster.

"He could be anywhere," I said.

"I *know*," said Iggy. "We'll *never* find him!"

We searched for ages, in the bookshelf, behind the piano, in the laundry basket, under our beds.

"*Gruffles*," we whispered. "*Come out wherever you are.*"

"What's going on?" Dad said. He was on his way downstairs to make coffee.

"We're looking for Gruffles," I said.

Dad said, "Oh," and carried on going. Then he stopped. "What do you mean, you're looking for him?" he said.

Iggy didn't say anything. She bit her lip and stood with her toes together and played with her hands.

"We can't find him," I said, and my voice was a bit croaky because I was scared of getting told off. "He's escaped."

Dad was very awake suddenly. "He can't have done," he said. Dad went to have a look in the cage. "Did you leave the door open?" he said.

Iggy shrugged and pulled a face and wouldn't look at him.

"I don't know," I said. "I don't remember."

"Brilliant," said Dad. "B–rilliant."

"What's brilliant?" said Mum, smiling and expecting good news.

"They've lost the school hamster," Dad said. "The school hamster is at large."

"At large?" said Iggy? "He's like *that big*," and she put her hands apart to show how not-large Gruffles was.

"No," said Dad. "He's loose, he's free, he's wandering about. He's *missing*."

"What are we going to tell Rwaida?" I said. I was starting to really worry about that.

"We're not going to tell her anything," said Mum. "We are going to find it."

"It?" said Iggy. "*It?* Gruffles is a *he*."

"Then we're going to find *him*," said Mum. "There is no way we are losing a hamster that doesn't belong to us. It is not happening."

"It just did," said Dad.

"Not helpful," Mum said.

We looked all day. We put hamster food in corners and we listened carefully for scuttling and we looked in places only a hamster could squeeze into.

Iggy was a rubbish searcher. She kept wandering off and pretending to look in her room.

Dad said, "Why isn't she helping? It's her responsibility."

Mum said, "Just leave her."

Gruffles was nowhere. "What are we going to do?" I said.

Dad pulled a face and shook his head. Mum closed her eyes and sighed. Iggy shrugged again.

I said, "Will we have to own up?" I didn't want to go into school in the morning and say we'd lost him. I was very scared about doing that.

"Or we could get another hamster and replace it and not tell anybody," said Dad.

"Bad idea," said Mum.

"Of course it is," said Dad.

Iggy didn't say anything.

"Maybe he'll just come back in the night while we're sleeping," I said. "Maybe one of us should stay up all night and watch for him."

"I will," said Iggy.

"No you won't," said Dad.

At bedtime I lay and listened to the sound of Gruffles not rattling around on his little wheel and not digging about in his sawdust. It was very quiet. Missing hamster quiet.

And then I heard a sound.

The sound was Iggy. She was talking really quietly in a whisper. I couldn't hear what she was saying, but I could hear her through the wall.

"Who are you talking to?" I said.

"No one," said Iggy.

She was quiet for a bit, but then I heard her again. It was her special, extra gentle voice. The voice she used for talking to teddies and babies and kittens and puppies. And hamsters.

I got out of bed and crept along the landing so Iggy wouldn't hear me. I put my eye to the crack of her door like a proper spy.

She was sitting on her bed with a shoebox.
She had her hands in it. She was smiling at it.
Then she lifted something out of it.

Gruffles.

She kissed his nose and gave him her best
smile.

"Iggy!" I said.

Iggy jumped.

She dropped the hamster.

Gruffles scuttled under her bed.

We got down on the floor to look for him.

"You stole Gruffles," I said.

"I didn't mean to," she said.

"You can't steal him," I said.

"I don't want to give him back," she said. "I *love* him!"

"I love him too," I said. "I don't want to give him back either. But we can't steal him. We'll be in big trouble."

"I can't own up now," Iggy said. "Everyone searched all day. I'm in big trouble anyway."

"Where is he?" I said. "Can you see him?"

Iggy wriggled a bit further under the bed. "He's here," she said, and she giggled. "He's reading one of my magazines."

"We mustn't let him get away," I said. "Don't make any sudden movements."

We got closer to Gruffles really slowly. He seemed quite happy under the bed. He didn't seem too worried about us creeping up on him.

When we were really close, I reached out and grabbed him.

"Gotcha!" I said, and Iggy squealed with excitement.

"What's going on up there?" Mum called up the stairs.

"Nothing!" we said at the same time.

"Don't make me come up!" she said.

"We won't," I said back, and Iggy put her hand over her mouth to stop doing any more squealing.

"Let's pretend he came back on his own," I said. "I won't tell."

"Promise?" said Iggy.

"Promise."

"OK," she whispered. "You do it," and she gave me the shoebox she'd hidden Gruffles in. "I don't want that any more either," she said.

I crept out on to the landing where Gruffles's cage was glinting in the dark. I had him in a firm grip because I definitely did not want to drop him now and let him escape for real. I put him back in his cage and I shut the door properly, and then I hid the shoebox in the laundry basket and went to bed.

"I did it," I said to Iggy through the wall.

"OK," she said back.

I fell asleep listening to Gruffles rattling and digging just like normal.

In the morning, Iggy and me acted all surprised. "He's back!" we shouted, and we rushed to tell Mum and Dad and we danced about the kitchen.

"He came back *all by himself*," Iggy said.

"All by himself?" Mum said, and I said, "Yes, isn't he *clever*?"

Dad said Gruffles was more than clever. He was actually a genius. "Not only did he find his way home," he said, "but he also managed to shut the door behind him. *That* is a special hamster."

"We know he's special," Iggy said. "That's why we *love* him."

We ate breakfast, and everyone was happy and relieved because the school hamster wasn't missing after all and nobody was going to be in trouble.

I went upstairs and made my bed and took my pyjamas to the laundry basket.

It was empty.

No laundry.

No shoebox.

That meant Mum or Dad must have found it and must have known. But they never said.

And even though Iggy and me asked and asked, Gruffles never came to stay with us again.

**About the author**

Jenny Valentine moved house every two years when she was growing up. She worked in a wholefood shop in Primrose Hill for fifteen years where she met many extraordinary people and sold more organic loaves than there are words in her first novel, *Finding Violet Park*, which won the Guardian Children's Fiction Prize. The *Iggy and Me* books are her first titles for younger readers.

## About the illustrator

Joe Berger grew up in Bristol, where he did an Art
Foundation Course before moving to London in
1991. He works as a freelance illustrator and
animator, and also co-writes and illustrates a
weekly comic strip in the *Guardian*. His first picture
book, *Bridget Fidget*, was nominated for the
Booktrust Early Years Award.